W9-BNT-533

the CRiTTeR club

All About Ellie

by Callie Barkley ♥ illustrated by Marsha Riti

LITTLE SIMON
New York London Toronto Sydney New Delhi

LITTLE SIMON

An imprint of Simon & Schuster Children's Publishing Division 1230 Avenue of the Americas, New York, New York 10020 Copyright © 2013 by Simon & Schuster, Inc. All rights reserved, including the right of reproduction in whole or in part in any form. LITTLE SIMON is a registered trademark of Simon & Schuster, Inc., and associated colophon is a trademark of Simon & Schuster, Inc. For information about special discounts for bulk purchases, please contact Simon & Schuster Special Sales at 1-866-506-1949 or business@simonandschuster.com. The Simon & Schuster Speakers Bureau can bring authors to your live event. For more information or to book an event contact the Simon & Schuster Speakers Bureau at 1-866-248-3049 or visit our website at www.simonspeakers.com. Designed by Laura Roode

Manufactured in the United States of America 1112 FFG

First Edition 10 9 8 7 6 5 4 3 2 1

Library of Congress Cataloging-in-Publication Data Barkley, Callie. All about Ellie / by Callie Barkley ; illustrated by Marsha Riti. — 1st ed. p. cm. — (The Critter Club ; #2) Summary: When she wins the lead role in a school play, second-grader Ellie neglects her friends in the Critter Club and their new animal shelter. [1. Friendship—Fiction. 2. Clubs—Fiction. 3. Animal shelters—Fiction. 4. Theater—Fiction.] I. Riti, Marsha, ill. II. Title. PZ7.B250585Al 2013 [Fic]—dc23 2012006295

ISBN 978-1-4424-5788-1 (pbk)

ISBN 978-1-4424-5789-8 (hc)

ISBN 978-1-4424-5790-4 (eBook)

Table of Contents

Chapter 1

Starring . . . Ellie!

"Okay," said Ellie, kneeling on her bed. "Here's what I planned for us to do tonight!"

Her best friends, Liz, Amy, and Marion, had just arrived. Ellie was so excited. It was Friday and her turn to host their weekly sleepover.

"First I can teach you this really cool dance I learned in tap class,"

Ellie began. "And after that we can put on the play we made up at Liz's house! And—"

"Ellie, hold on," Liz said with a giggle. "We just got here!"

"Yeah," agreed Marion. She unrolled her sleeping bag. "All that sounds fun, but maybe we could relax and talk first?"

Ellie's face fell a little. She'd been looking forward to this sleepover for . . . well, *forever*. After all, she only got a turn to host every four weeks, and being the host was special. It meant planning everything and being at the center of it all!

"Oh!" said Amy. "We have some Critter Club stuff to talk about. Remember?"

Ellie got excited again. "The bunnies!" she cried.

"Right," said Amy. "Our first

animals at The Critter Club!"

Ellie and her friends had been working hard to get The Critter Club up and running. A few weeks ago it was an empty barn belonging to Ms. Sullivan, their new friend. Now, with the help of Amy's mom, veterinarian Dr. Purvis, it was an animal shelter. It had all been Ms. Sullivan's idea!

Before The Critter Club the girls thought Ms. Sullivan was kind of mean, but they'd been totally wrong. When Ms. Sullivan's puppy Rufus had gone missing, the girls helped her find him. That's when The Critter Club was born!

"You still don't know who left the bunnies?" Marion asked Amy.

Amy shook her head no. "There was no note," Amy replied. "Just

three baby bunnies in a card-
board box."

"Poor things!" said Ellie. "How
could someone just leave them?"

Amy shrugged. "Mom thinks
someone's pet rabbit had babies,
and they couldn't take care of
them all."

"Well, speaking of taking care of them," said Marion, pulling out a notebook, "we should make a schedule." Marion was super organized. She was always writing things down and making lists.

Ellie hopped off her bed. She sat on the floor next to Marion. In her notebook Marion made a chart.

"So we'll take turns," said Marion. "Each day after school two of us will go feed the bunnies and give them water. Amy's mom and Ms. Sullivan will handle the morning shifts."

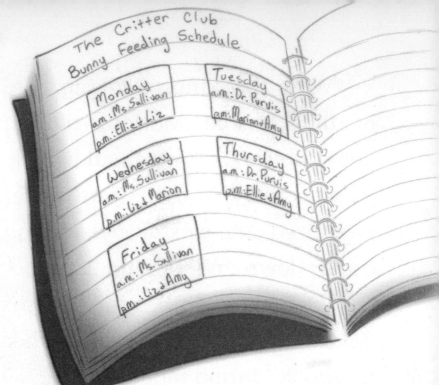

The Critter Club
Bunny Feeding Schedule

Monday
a.m.: Ms. Sullivan
p.m.: Elliet Liz

Tuesday
a.m.: Dr. Purvis
p.m.: Marion & Amy

Wednesday
a.m.: Ms. Sullivan
p.m.: Liz & Marion

Thursday
a.m.: Dr. Purvis
p.m.: Ellie & Amy

Friday
a.m.: Ms. Sullivan
p.m.: Liz & Amy

All the girls agreed. Liz picked up a pen. She drew three little bunnies below the chart.

"We have to find good homes for them," Ellie said. "They're counting on us, and we can't let them down!" Then she jumped up. "Okay, now, on to other things . . ."

Ellie ducked behind her hot-pink window curtains. She peeked out at her friends. "Who's trying out for the spring play?" she asked.

Their school, Santa Vista Elementary,

put on a play every year. This year's musical was called *Miss Ladybug Saves Spring*.

"We should all try out!" Ellie cried excitedly.

"Not me," said Liz. "I'm finishing my paint-ing for that big art con-test, remember?" Liz was an amazing artist. "Plus, you guys know I can't sing!" she added with a laugh.

Marion pulled her long brown hair into a ponytail. "I'm way

too busy too," she said. "Homework plus piano lessons three times a week!"

Ellie sighed. "How about you, Amy?" she asked. But Ellie knew what Amy was about to say.

"Me? Get on stage? In front of *people*? And *dance*? No way," Amy said, shaking her head.

Liz smiled a little smile. "How about you, Ellie? Are *you* going to try out?"

"YES!!!" Ellie squealed. She

jumped out from behind the curtain. "I can't wait! Have you seen the stage? It's sooooo big! Do you think they'll have the spotlight on for auditions? Oh! What should I wear? What song should I sing? You guys have to help me decide!"

Liz, Marion, and Amy laughed. They settled in, happy to be Ellie's audience. Ellie was so glad they were there to cheer her on and help her prepare.

After all, that's what friends were for. Right?

Chapter 2

Ellie Takes the Stage

Backstage at the school auditorium, Ellie looked at herself in the mirror. It was the big day, and Ellie was next on the list. Mrs. Jameson, the teacher who ran drama club, would call her name any minute to audition for the lead role! That part almost always went to a third grader, but Ellie felt she *had* to try for it anyway. Obviously, Miss Ladybug's costume would be red. *Red is totally my color!* thought Ellie.

"Ellie Mitchell," she said to herself, "this is your chance." She fluffed her hair and smoothed her red dress. All her life—all eight years—she had wanted to be a star. At two years old, she dressed up

and did shows for her mom and dad. At three years old, she started dance classes. She remembered a video her mom took of her first tap recital. In it she had bumped into another girl to be in the spotlight.

Just then Ellie heard Mrs. Jameson calling. "Ellie! Ellie Mitchell!"

It was time for her to take center stage. Getting the lead role would be her dream come true! "You can do this!" Ellie told herself. She hurried onstage.

The stage lights were bright. Squinting, Ellie could make out Mrs. Jameson in the front row. She saw someone waving from the back row.

It was Liz! And Marion and Amy were next to her! They had come to

cheer her on! *Aw, that's so sweet of them*, thought Ellie. *They're such great friends.*

"Hello, Ellie," Mrs. Jameson said kindly. "Whenever you are ready, I'd love to hear your audition song."

Ellie took a deep breath. Her eyes locked on Liz, Marion, and Amy.

She pretended she was in her own bedroom and that she was singing to them—just to them. The next moment she was lost in the song. Her voice filled the auditorium as she moved to the music. She even threw in some twirls, leaps, and hand motions.

It was over before Ellie knew it. Her last note hung in the air, ringing clear and strong.

Then another sound filled the air—a wonderful sound. Applause! In the back row Liz, Marion, and Amy were clapping like crazy. Ellie took a bow and waved at her friends.

VIBs:
Very Important Bunnies

The next day after school the girls walked together to Mrs. Jameson's classroom. She had posted the cast list outside her door. It listed the role each person had been given.

There was Ellie's name, right at the top!

Miss Ladybug Saves Spring	
∽ Role ∽	∽ Student ∽
Miss Ladybug	Ellie Mitchell
Bumblebee 1	Steven Connor
Bumblebee 2	Karlie Lemon
Flower Dancer 1	Marjorie Jones

23

Ellie was so excited and surprised! She was speechless. She—a second grader—would star as Miss Ladybug, the biggest role in the whole play!

Liz, Marion, and Amy each gave her a big hug. "Way to go, Ellie!" Liz squealed.

Ellie was in heaven. She was so happy she felt like she was walking on air. Then it slowly began to dawn on her: She had so much to do to get ready for the show!

* * * ° * * * * * * * * * * ♥ * * * *

Weeks flew by in a flash. Ellie had never felt so busy before.

Each school day during lunch hour, Mrs. Jameson held short rehearsals in the auditorium. Every Wednesday after school, they had a longer rehearsal.

Ellie also had Critter Club duty two days a week after school. On

Mondays she went with Liz. On Thursdays she and Amy went together.

It was enough to make Ellie's head spin! Luckily, Marion had made Ellie a schedule. She kept it taped to the front of her homework folder.

And that was just weekdays! On Saturdays and Sundays all four girls met at The Critter Club to feed the bunnies and clean the big rabbit hutch.

One sunny Saturday morning they were all in the barn. Marion

Weekly Schedule

Monday	Play rehearsal at lunchtime
	Critter Club with Liz in the afternoon
Tuesday	Play rehearsal at lunchtime
	After-school Dance!
Wednesday	Play rehearsal at lunchtime
	Play rehearsal (long one) after school
Thursday	Play rehearsal at lunchtime
	Critter Club with Amy in the afternoon
Friday	Play rehearsal at lunchtime
	Sleepover!!! Yay! ☆☆

sat on the floor with the bunnies playing around her.

"Is *that* the one we named Floppy?" Ellie asked, pointing to a gray bunny.

"No, that's Fluffy," said Amy.

She was hosing down the inside of the hutch. "The other gray one is Floppy."

"Which other gray one?" asked Ellie. She opened a bag of wood shavings to make fresh bedding. "Aren't they all gray?"

Liz giggled as she swept around

the rabbit hutch. "No, Frosty is sil-
very white. The light gray one is
Fluffy. And the steel gray one is
Floppy."

Marion and Amy laughed.
"Leave it to the artist to have three
different names for the same color!"
Marion said.

Ellie felt badly that she hadn't known which bunny was which. She hadn't been there when Amy's mom had given the bunnies full checkups. Dr. Purvis had also taught the other girls the basics of caring for them. Bunnies loved to be petted. They were calm and gentle, but their nails could be sharp. Bunnies sometimes chewed on things they shouldn't. The girls could give them special chew toys

or carrots to chew instead.

Amy's mom said that people looking for a new pet might not even think of rabbits. It was up to The Critter Club to change that and find homes for their furry friends!

But right now all Ellie could think about was how much more play practice she needed.

33

Chapter 4

One-Track Mind

There was so much going on! Ellie made sure to keep her friends up to date on *everything*. She jumped at any chance to tell them *all* about the play.

One morning Ellie was walking to school with Amy. Amy was talking about her weekend at her dad's house in Orange Blossom. Orange

Blossom was a bigger city near Santa Vista.

Meanwhile Ellie had a thought. She wanted to tell Amy about her costume for the play. It had long, flowing sleeves that looked like ladybug wings. The red fabric looked glittery

under the lights. When Ellie twirled around the stage . . .

"Ellie? Hello? Ellie?" Amy was saying.

"Oh, huh?" Ellie replied. "What did you say?"

"I was telling you all about my weekend at my dad's," Amy said. "It was really—"

"I'm *so* sorry, Amy!" Ellie jumped in. "I was thinking about my costume for the play!" She went on to tell Amy everything about her costume from head to toe.

Ellie saw Amy roll her eyes. She wasn't sure why. Maybe Amy had something *in* her eye? So Ellie kept on talking. She made sure not to leave anything out.

Another day Ellie was on the phone with Liz. "I forgot our reading book at school," Liz said. "Can I borrow yours?"

"Sure!" Ellie replied. "Come over! While you're here, I can read you my lines from the play! And you haven't heard my part in the opening song! I'll sing that for you

too. *And* I've got to tell you what happened at rehearsal today!"

"Um, actually," Liz said, "I bet Amy has her book at home. Her house is closer. I'll borrow hers. Thanks." And she hung up. *Guess she's in a hurry to do her homework,* thought Ellie.

Two days later at Marion's house,

Marion was telling Ellie a story about her horse, Coco. Right in the middle of it, Marion stopped. "Ellie, are you even listening?" she asked.

"What?" said Ellie. "What do you mean?"

"Well, you were humming," Marion said, "while I was talking."

"I was?" Ellie said. She *had* been thinking about a song from the play. She didn't realize she'd been singing it *out loud.* Ellie giggled. "Oops. It's just a song from the play. Want to hear it?"

Marion frowned. "Oh," she said. "Yes. *My* story can wait. Let's hear *your* song."

"Okay!" said Ellie, and she began to sing. If her friends couldn't be in the play with her, she was glad she could tell them all about it!

"Ladybug Sunshine, la, la, la!"

Chapter 5

Preshow Jitters!

The next Friday before school Ellie checked the calendar. The play was exactly one week away!

At school, before the morning bell, the girls met up on the playground. "Do you know what today is?" Ellie asked them.

"Yep!" said Liz. "Friday!"

"We have a sleepover tonight!"

Amy cheered. "Marion, it's at your house, right?"

Marion nodded and opened her mouth to speak. But Ellie blurted out, "No! Not that! I mean, the play! The play is in *one* week—one week from *today*!"

Liz put her arm around Ellie. "Don't worry," she said in a calm tone. "You're going to be great."

"You're totally ready," said Marion.

"We've heard all the lines to all the songs . . . ," said Amy. "You *definitely* know them by heart!"

Ellie smiled. "I know, I know," she said. "Oh yeah! I almost forgot to tell you guys. I can't make it to the sleepover tonight."

"What?" Liz asked, surprised. "Why not?"

Ellie sat down on a swing. "I really need to use *all* my spare time to prepare for the show— study my lines, and rehearse my songs, and get a ton of rest," said Ellie. "It's going to be a busy weekend. We have an extra rehearsal tomorrow morning. Then my mom is taking me to Orange Blossom to pick up my specially made costume!" Going shopping in Orange Blossom was always a special treat.

"Wait," said Amy. "So you're not coming to the sleepover *and* you won't be at The Critter Club tomorrow?"

The Critter Club! thought Ellie, remembering. She shook her head and shrugged. "I can't make it," she said. "It's just . . . the play is only *a week away. Just seven days.*"

Marion rolled her eyes. "Uh, yeah. You mentioned *that.*"

Just then the bell rang. Everyone had to line up to go inside. That got Ellie thinking. At the end of the play would the cast line up to take a bow together? Or would they each get to take their own bow? She had to ask Mrs. Jameson about that at rehearsal.

Chapter 6

Ellie's Fan Club

"Ellie!" called Mrs. Mitchell. "Time for dinner!"

It was Sunday evening. In her room Ellie sighed. She dropped her script and went downstairs. She stood next to her seat at the dining room table. Ellie's mom, dad, little brother Toby, and Nana Gloria were already there, waiting for her.

"Mom, I don't have time to eat," Ellie said.

"Oh, come on, Ellie," her mom replied. "You have to eat *something*."

"Your mother's right," said Nana Gloria. "You need to keep up your strength. Otherwise you'll never make it to Friday's showtime!" She

winked and smiled at Ellie. Ellie smiled back. She was so happy Nana Gloria had come to live with them a few weeks ago. Already, Ellie couldn't remember what the house was like without her. She always gave good advice.

Her dad picked up a covered dish. "You've been going nonstop all weekend, Ellie," he said. "So sit, relax, and eat. We made your favorite." He whisked the lid off the dish.

"Chicken pot pie!" Ellie cried. *Mmm,* she thought. *I am kind of hungry.* She sat down next to Toby.

"Yummy!" said Toby, picking up his fork.

"Bravo!" came a squawky voice from the corner. Everyone laughed and looked at Nana Gloria's parrot, Lenny, perched in his cage. Ellie and Lenny had become good pals. Ellie had taught him to say "Bravo!" after she sang and danced.

"Can Lenny come to the play, please?" asked Toby. "And Sam, too?" Sam was their golden retriever. Toby didn't like going places without Sam.

Ellie laughed at the thought of barks and a squawky "Bravo!" mixed in with the applause. "I don't think so, Toby," she said.

Plus, adorable critters would totally steal the spotlight! Ellie thought.

Squawk!

Squawk!

Chapter 7

A Bad Kind of Drama

On Monday at school, Ellie spotted Amy and Marion heading into the classroom. "Guys! Wait up!" she called and hurried over.

"Oh, hey, Ellie," Marion said flatly.

"Hi," said Amy.

They both sounded kind of bored to Ellie. They kept on walking.

"Hey, what's up?" Ellie said excitedly. "I haven't seen you guys all weekend! How was the sleepover? How was Saturday at The Critter Club?" Ellie went on without really waiting for an answer. "Boy, what a crazy weekend I had! Rehearsal, costume fitting, studying my lines—"

"That's nice, Ellie," Marion said in the same flat voice.

"Yeah, sounds great," said Amy.

That's funny, thought Ellie. *They don't sound like they think it's nice and great.*

Their teacher, Mrs. Sienna, asked everyone to take their seats. Without another word Amy and Marion crossed the room. They sat at their desks by the window. Ellie saw Liz already in her seat by the bookshelf. Ellie waved. Liz waved back, but didn't smile. *That's not like Liz,* thought Ellie.

I wonder if she's feeling okay.

Ellie sat down at her desk near the classroom door. Soon Mrs. Sienna got them started on morning math, but Ellie couldn't concentrate on fractions. She kept looking over at her friends. They all had their noses in their work. Ellie tried to catch their attention, but none of

them looked her way all morning.

It was almost lunchtime when there was a knock on the classroom door. Mrs. Sienna answered it. A fifth grader gave the teacher a folded piece of paper. "Liz," she said after reading it, "the principal would like to see you."

Ellie looked at Liz. She looked surprised. "Right now?" Liz asked.

"Yes, right now," said Mrs. Sienna.

"Take your lunch. You can go straight to the cafeteria afterward."

Uh-oh, thought Ellie. *What's up?* She watched Liz get her lunch from her backpack. Then she walked out of the classroom.

Ten long minutes later the lunch

bell rang. Ellie jumped out of her seat, got out her lunch bag, and headed for the door. Ellie wanted to talk to Marion and Amy. She caught up to them in the hallway.

"Guys," she said, "is everything okay with Liz?"

Marion and Amy kept on walking. Ellie thought they hadn't heard her.

"Guys?" Ellie tried again.

Marion stopped and turned to Ellie. "Oh! Are you speaking to us, *superstar*?"

Ellie froze in her tracks. Usually,

she loved being called a superstar. But not the way Marion had said it. That way sounded more like a bad word.

Ellie didn't know what to say. She felt her cheeks getting hot. She wasn't sure what from. Anger? Embarrassment? Ellie looked at Amy, who only looked at the ground.

Ellie opened her mouth. She wanted to say something back, but nothing came out. She closed it, turned, and stomped away.

During lunchtime rehearsal in the auditorium, Ellie was surrounded by her new friends from the play, but all she could think of was her old ones.

Suddenly, Ellie didn't feel like talking about the play.

Were Marion and Amy jealous of her? And what was up with Liz?

An Ellie
Sometimes Forgets

Outside, after school, Ellie didn't wait for Marion or Amy, and Liz was nowhere to be seen.

Where is she? Ellie wondered, walking home alone. *How could she abandon me at a time like this?* Ellie wanted to ask Liz about Marion and Amy. After all, Ellie was the star of the play. She got to wear a glittery costume. She had lots of new friends. They must be jealous. Ellie was sure that's why Marion had said what she did.

When Ellie got home, she went to her room. Her Miss Ladybug costume was hanging on the closet door. *It really is so beautiful!* Ellie thought. *Maybe trying it on will cheer me up.*

For a couple of minutes it worked.

Ellie looked at herself in the mirror and smiled. She twirled and posed. She said some of her lines. She sang one of her songs. *This is what I'll look like up on stage!* she thought.

Then the feeling faded. Ellie remembered that awful way

Marion's voice sounded. She remembered the look on Amy's face. Quickly, she changed into her regular clothes. She flopped onto her bed. Suddenly, Ellie didn't feel excited about the play at all.

Just then the phone rang. Nana Gloria called up from downstairs: "Ellie! It's for you! It's Liz."

Finally! Ellie thought. *A friendly voice!* She flew down the stairs and ran to the phone. "Liz! Where have you been?" Ellie asked, out of breath. "I looked for you after school!"

Ellie waited for Liz to answer in

her usual easygoing way, but there was just silence at the other end.

"Liz? Liz!" Ellie said.

"I'm here, Ellie," Liz replied. Her voice was quiet and sounded . . .

different . . . like she wasn't smiling.

"Where were you at school today?" Ellie asked. She decided to skip to the important stuff. "You won't believe how mean Marion and Amy were to me today! They barely talked to me or looked at me. And then Marion called me 'superstar'! I think they are jealous of the whole play thing. I mean—"

"Ellie!" Liz shouted. Ellie stopped talking. "Did you forget anything today?" Liz asked her.

Forget anything? Ellie thought. She ran through things in her mind. She had her homework and reading book. She'd gone to play rehearsal. Oh! She still needed to try new hairstyles for the play. Plus she wanted to ask her mom if she could wear lipstick. . . .

"It's *Monday*!" said Liz, hinting.

"*Our* day? After school? At The Critter Club? You forgot to meet me at the barn after school, Ellie. I took care of everything all by myself!"

Ellie gasped. The bunnies! How had she forgotten?

She heard Liz sigh at the other

end. "This play—it's all you can think about!" Liz said. "It's bad enough that you forgot about the bunnies, but what about your best friend?"

Ellie felt a terrible sinking feeling in her stomach, but Liz wasn't done. "And in case you care, my painting won first place in the art contest. That's why the principal wanted to see me. It's going on to the state competition. You're not the only one who has exciting stuff happening, Ellie. Even if you've been acting like it!"

Liz hung up the phone before Ellie could answer. It was just as well, because, for once, Ellie didn't know what to say.

Chapter 9

A Secret Movie Star

Ellie felt a lump rising in her throat. She wanted to get out of the house. She didn't feel like telling her family why she was upset.

"I'm going for a bike ride!" she called into the kitchen.

"Okay!" Nana Gloria replied as the screen door slammed. In seconds, Ellie was riding away

79

down the street.

At first she had no destination in mind. Then, suddenly, she wanted to visit the bunnies. She steered her bike toward Ms. Sullivan's place.

Ten minutes later Ellie was in the barn. Fluffy was in her lap. Frosty was sniffing her shoe. *Or is that one Floppy?* Ellie wondered. The third bunny was poking his head into her jacket pocket.

"I'm really sorry, bunnies," she

whispered to them. "I'm sorry I forgot you today." Tears welled up in
her eyes. She couldn't hold it in.
Ellie petted Fluffy as she cried and
cried.

"Ellie?" came a voice at the door.
Ellie turned. Ms. Sullivan was peeking into the barn.

"What's the matter?" She came over and wrapped an arm around Ellie. "Is everything okay?"

Ellie wiped her eyes on a sleeve. "Yes, Ms. Sullivan," she sniffed. "It's just—" The sobs came again and Ellie couldn't speak.

"Come on, dear," said Ms. Sullivan.

"Come in the house with me."

Ellie nodded. Together they put the bunnies back in the hutch. Then they walked across Ms. Sullivan's wide backyard and went in the back door of her gigantic gingerbread house.

As Ellie sat down in Ms. Sullivan's kitchen, Rufus came running in. He jumped up, resting his head and front paws on Ellie's knee. Ellie petted him while Ms. Sullivan got her some milk

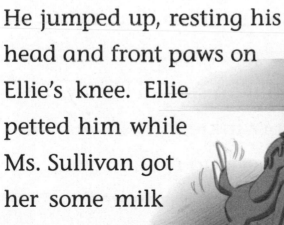

and cookies. By the time she set them on the table, Ellie had stopped crying.

Ellie explained about the play. She told Ms. Sullivan what Marion and Liz had said. She described the look on Amy's face.

"I guess I *have* been really focused on the play," said Ellie. "It just . . . it means a lot to me. Can't they see that?"

Ms. Sullivan smiled kindly. Then she got a twinkle in her eye. "Ellie, I have something to show you," she said. "Wait here a minute."

Ms. Sullivan left the room. Rufus stretched out under the table, waiting for cookie crumbs. When Ms. Sullivan returned, she had a photo in her hand. She handed it to Ellie.

Ruby Fairchild

Strangely,
the woman in the photo
looked familiar to Ellie, but where
had Ellie seen her before?

"As you know," said Ms. Sullivan.
"I haven't always lived in Santa
Vista. Before I moved here, I lived
in Hollywood."

Hollywood, California, thought Ellie, *where movies are made.* "Movies! That's it!" cried Ellie. "Have I seen this woman in a movie? In an older movie like the ones Nana Gloria likes to watch?"

Ms. Sullivan nodded. "Yes. That woman was a famous actress. Her screen name was Ruby Fairchild."

"Yeah! Ruby Fairchild!" said Ellie, looking again at the photo. "She was in *The Lost Sheep.* We watched it the other night!" Ellie looked up at Ms. Sullivan. "Why do you have her picture?" Ellie gasped.

"Did you *know* her in Hollywood?"

Ms. Sullivan laughed. "You could say that, Ellie," she said. "You see, Ruby Fairchild is . . . me!"

Ellie stared at Ms. Sullivan. Then she stared at the photo. "That's *you*!" she cried. "She *does* look like you!"

"Well, a much younger me," Ms. Sullivan said with a smile.

Ellie was amazed. She listened as Ms. Sullivan told her about her life in Hollywood. It sounded like Ellie's idea of heaven! The movie stars! The fancy parties! The awards! Signing autographs for crowds of cheering fans!

"I had a great career," said Ms. Sullivan, "but when I stopped making movies, I was ready for a quieter life. That's when I moved to Santa Vista." Ms. Sullivan sighed. "I thought if people here knew me as Ruby Fairchild, I'd never be left

alone. So I hid who I was and kept to myself. I didn't go out much, and I even lost touch with most of my old friends. A lot of days I was all alone in this giant house," she smiled, "until I got Rufus." She looked down at the big puppy under the table.

"Woof!" Rufus replied. His tail thumped against a chair leg.

"Then Rufus went missing, and you girls helped me find him," Ms. Sullivan went on. "Before The Critter Club, I hadn't made new friends in years!"

Ms. Sullivan put her arm around Ellie. "It's important to be kind to your friends. Keep them close. And here's a piece of advice, from one actress to another." Ellie grinned. Ruby Fairchild was calling *her* an actress? "Good friends will be there for you, but it can't *always* be about you."

Ellie finished her milk and cookies. Then Ms. Sullivan showed her more of her Hollywood stuff—old movie posters, scripts, and photos.

"Nana Gloria would flip to see all this!" Ellie said. "But don't you worry. Your secret will be safe with me, Ruby Fairchild—Ms. *Sullivan,* I mean."

Making Things Right

Ellie rode home on her bike, thinking the whole way. She felt a lot better, thanks to Ms. Sullivan. She still dreamed of being a star, but she realized something important. Being a star would mean very little without friends.

"Dinner in fifteen minutes, Ellie!" Ellie's mom called as she came in the front door.

"Okay!" replied Ellie, running upstairs. She had just enough time. She needed to get some things down on paper.

In her room Ellie sat down at her desk. She took out three sheets of her special stationery. She chose a pretty red pen and began to write a note to Liz.

Ellie wrote a similar note to Marion

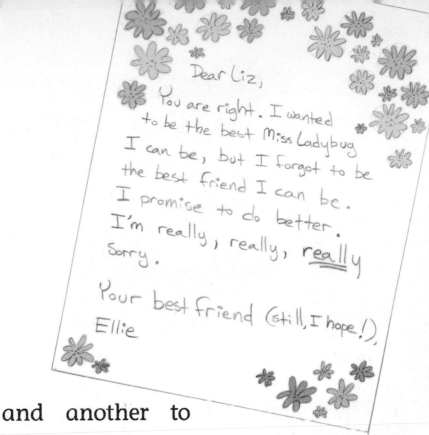

Dear Liz,

You are right. I wanted to be the best Miss Ladybug I can be, but I forgot to be the best friend I can be. I promise to do better. I'm really, really, really sorry.

Your best friend (still, I hope!),

Ellie

and another to Amy. She selected a special sticker to seal each envelope. Next she wrote her friends' names on the front of each envelope.

Feeling hopeful, Ellie tucked the

notes into her backpack. Then she headed downstairs for dinner.

* * * * • ✿ * * * * * * • * * * * ❤ •

The next morning Ellie got to school a little early and left the notes on her friends' desks. Then she sat down at her own desk and took out a book.

Ellie pretended to read it, but

really she was peeking over the top.
When Liz came in, Ellie watched
her go to her desk. She saw the note
and opened it. She was reading it!

Oh, what's she thinking? Ellie wondered.

She didn't
have to won-
der very long.
Liz looked over

at Ellie. Slowly, a warm smile spread across Liz's face. Ellie smiled back.

Mrs. Sienna was starting class, but Ellie watched Marion and Amy read their notes, too. Amy smiled and gave Ellie a thumbs-up. Marion looked over and mouthed some words to Ellie.

"I'm sorry, too," she was saying.

Ellie nodded and smiled. She let out a happy sigh. It was like a weight had been lifted off of her.

The morning sped by. At

lunchtime Ellie met up with her friends in the hallway.

"Can you forgive me?" she asked them.

"Of course, Ellie!" said Liz. The girls wrapped Ellie in a big group hug.

"We're like sisters," said Amy.

Marion nodded. "Even sisters argue sometimes, but they always make up."

Ellie beamed. "Well, then, I have a favor to ask," she said. She looked at Liz. "Can I come over after school? I'd love to see your prizewinning painting. I'm so proud of you, Liz!"

"Oh yes!" cried Marion. "You

have to see it! She got a blue first-place ribbon and everything!"

Liz laughed.

"Yes, of course. You can definitely come over and see it."

"I can't wait!" Ellie cried. "Oh! I almost forgot to tell you guys! I had an idea. It's about the bunnies. I think I know how to get people to adopt them!"

Chapter 11

Bravo, Ellie!

The Santa Vista Elementary School auditorium was packed. It was Friday night—the night of the big play, *Miss Ladybug Saves Spring.*

The show sped by, number by number, and before long the play was almost over! Ellie and her cast mates had performed their roles perfectly. Now the red velvet curtain

opened one last time—for the big finale!

Flower dancers twirled around. Butterflies fluttered on tiptoe. Inchworms inched in time to the music. Dancing raindrops swung their legs up and down.

Last to come onstage was

Ellie—Miss Ladybug! She moved gracefully toward the front of the stage. The airy fabric of her sleeves fluttered behind her. There was something else behind her, too—a little red wagon. Miss Ladybug held its handle and pulled it along. Inside, munching on lettuce, were

three gray bunnies: Floppy, Fluffy, and Frosty!

From the audience came a great big "awwww."

Ellie slowly pulled the wagon across the stage. The audience read the sign on the wagon's side.

Then Ellie carefully handed the wagon to someone offstage.

The finale continued, building until the whole cast was onstage. They lined up in a row. One by one, each cast member took a bow. The crowd got to its feet, clapping and cheering.

As the lead, Ellie was the last to take her bow. The spotlight fell on her. She looked out into the audience. Everyone was there! She saw her mom and dad, Toby, and Nana Gloria, cheering. Behind them, Liz, Marion, and Amy waved at Ellie. Liz even whistled!

Then, from down in the first row, a figure approached the stage. It was Ms. Sullivan! She handed up

to Ellie a huge bouquet of red roses. "Bravo, Ellie!" she called out.

Ellie felt on top of the world. This was her moment. She had dreamed about it, but in her dreams, she had only seen herself.

The real moment was a million times better, and Ellie realized why. It was because her friends were there to share it with her.

Read on for a sneak peek at
the next Critter Club book:

Liz Learns a Lesson

Liz sat down on the bright green grass. She closed her eyes and soaked up the late afternoon sunshine. "Can you believe it?" she said to her friends Ellie, Amy, and Marion. "Tomorrow is the *last day of school!*"

"Hel-lo, summer!" Ellie cried joyfully. "Hello, ice cream and swimming and flip-flops—"

"And lots and lots of Critter Club!" added Amy.

The Critter Club was an animal rescue shelter the girls started. They got the idea from their friend, Ms. Sullivan, after the girls found her lost puppy, Rufus. Amy's mom, a veterinarian, was a huge help too. Together they had turned Ms. Sullivan's big, empty barn into a cozy shelter for lost and lonely animals.

Thanks to The Critter Club, three abandoned bunnies had new homes. Right now the Club had no animal guests . . . except for Rufus, of course!

That was about to change.

Marion opened her notebook. "We've already got ten families signed up for pet-sitting!" she said.

Ellie let out a happy squeal. "Yay! Amy's mom was right. Pet-sitting was such a great idea!"

"I think so too!" said Amy. "While families are away on summer vacation, their pets can stay here in Ms. Sullivan's barn!"

Liz flopped backward onto the soft, warm grass. She was *so* happy and excited! She'd get to spend lots of time with her friends, *and* she was done with homework until September!

The truth was that Liz sometimes had a hard time with school work— especially math. She would definitely *not* miss math over vacation.

The girls talked about their other summer plans. Marion was going to a music day camp for the month of July. She had been taking piano lessons since she was five.

Amy was going to help out at her mom's veterinary clinic. She also planned to spend a lot of weekends with her dad in Orange Blossom. "He just got a pool in his backyard," Amy said.

Ellie and her little brother Toby had fun plans with their grandmother, Nana Gloria. "She's going to take us to the library and the zoo and the Santa Vista pool!" Ellie said excitedly.

Liz sat up on the grass. "Well, guess what I'm doing?" she said.

"Art?" guessed Ellie, Amy, and Marion at the same time. All four girls started laughing.

"How did you guess?" Liz said with a grin. Of course, her friends knew she loved to paint and draw. Ms. Cummings's art room was Liz's favorite place at school. There, she never felt like the one who didn't "get it"—unlike in math class.

"Okay, you're right!" Liz said. "Ms. Cummings is teaching a class in July at the Santa Vista Library!" Liz glanced at Amy. "I'll look for you there?"

Amy giggled and nodded. "In the mystery section. I plan to read every *Nancy Drew* they've got, but first, I'll see you all at school tomorrow—for our last day!"

The girls hopped onto their bikes and headed to their homes for dinner.

Liz took a deep, happy breath as she pedaled. The warm air blew through her wavy blond hair.

Just one more day of school, she thought. *Then, let the summer begin!*